READING POWER

Earth Rocks!

Fossils

Holly Cefrey

The Rosen Publishing Group's
PowerKids Press™
New York

Published in 2003 by The Rosen Publishing Group, Inc.
29 East 21st Street, New York, NY 10010

First Edition

Book Design: Mindy Liu

Photo Credits: Cover, pp. 10–11 © Jonathan Blair/Corbis; p. 4 © Roger Garwood & Trish Ainslie/Corbis; pp. 5, 16–17 © Reuters NewMedia Inc./Corbis; p. 6 © Wolfgang Kaehler/Corbis; p. 7 © Paul A. Souders/Corbis; p. 8 © Breck P. Kent/Animals Animals; p. 9 © John Reader/SPL/Photo Researchers, Inc.; p. 12 © Marko Modic/Corbis; p. 13 © Harvey Lloyd/Getty Images; p. 14 © AP/Wide World Photos; p. 15 © Novosti/SPL/Photo Researchers, Inc.; p. 19 © Tom Bean/Corbis; p. 20 © Daniel LeClair/Getty Images; p. 21 © Newsmakers/Getty Images

Library of Congress Cataloging-in-Publication Data

Cefrey, Holly.
Fossils / Holly Cefrey.
    v. cm. — (Earth rocks!)
Summary: An introduction to fossils: what they are, how they form, what different kinds there are, where they're found, and how scientists learn from them.
Includes bibliographical references and index.
Contents: Fossils — How fossils form — Finding fossils — Learning from fossils.
ISBN 0-8239-6469-8 (library binding)
1. Fossils—Juvenile literature. [1. Fossils.] I. Title.
QE714.5 .C44 2003
560—dc21

                                        2002003387

Contents

Fossils

A fossil is the mark or the remains of a plant or an animal that lived long ago. People have found many fossils left by plants and animals that once lived on Earth. Some fossils are more than three billion years old.

The oldest fossils are of bacteria that lived about 3.5 billion years ago.

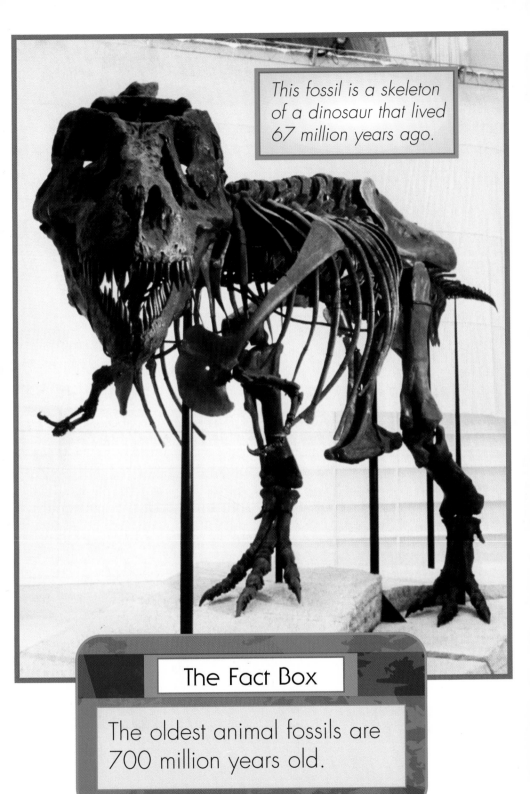

This fossil is a skeleton of a dinosaur that lived 67 million years ago.

The Fact Box

The oldest animal fossils are 700 million years old.

How Fossils Form

Most fossils are found in sedimentary rock. Sedimentary rock is made from layers of sand, stones, shells, and mud called sediment. When an animal or a plant dies, it may get buried in sediment. After thousands of years of being pressed together, the sediment and the remains of the plant or animal become rock.

For a plant to become a fossil in sedimentary rock, it must be covered with sediment before it rots.

Most fossils that are found are the bones of animals. The hair, skin, and soft parts of dead animals rot away.

The skeleton or bones of a dead animal in sedimentary rock may rot away over time. When this happens, a mold, or space, is left behind in the rock. The mold is in the shape of the dead animal. Also, an animal's feet or other body parts can leave prints in soft sediment. If these prints get hard, a mold is made.

This mold is of a trilobite (TRY-luh-byt). Trilobites lived more than 245 million years ago.

Footprints of early humans have been found.
These molds of footprints are 3.6 million years old.

Sometimes, water gets into a mold. The water may leave minerals in the mold. Over many years, the minerals grow in the mold to form a fossil in the shape of the animal. This kind of fossil is called a cast.

This cast is of two shellfish that lived more than 66 million years ago.

Fossils can also be made when minerals get inside a dead plant or animal that has been buried in mud. Over time, the minerals fill the dead plant or animal and replace its soft, inside parts. The minerals harden and take the plant or animal's shape.

Sometimes, fish are buried in the mud at the bottom of the ocean. Over time, minerals inside the fish turn to stone, forming fossils.

These fossilized pine trees were found in Arizona. The trees lived there about 225 million years ago.

13

Whole plants and animals can also become fossils. This can happen in places where the earth is frozen year-round or in places that are very hot and dry. When a plant or animal dies and is covered by ice or hot, dry sand, its body is protected from rotting. Air and water cannot harm the plant or animal's body.

These people are looking for fossils in tar. Tar comes from oil made under the earth's surface. Sometimes, animals that drank water covering a tar pit would get stuck in the tar, die, and become fossils.

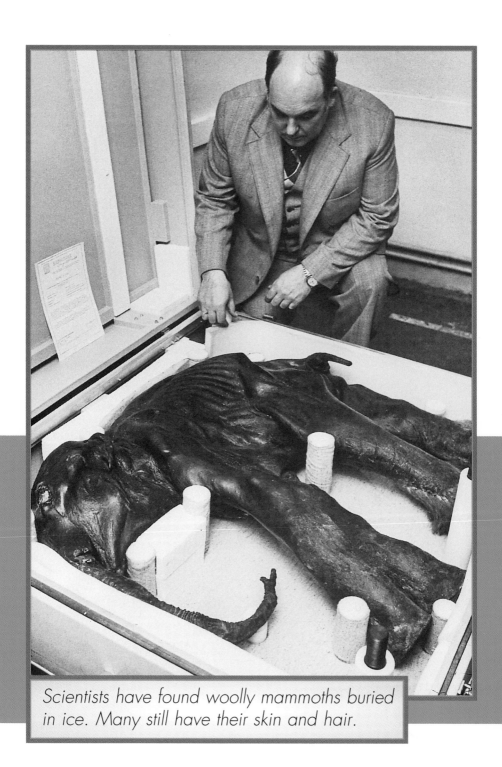

Scientists have found woolly mammoths buried in ice. Many still have their skin and hair.

Finding Fossils

Fossils are found all around the world. Sometimes, people find fossils when they dig in the ground to build roads or homes.

Scientists work slowly and use special tools to dig fossils from the earth.

Scientists also dig in places where they think fossils may be found. Scientists are careful not to harm fossils when digging them up.

Learning from Fossils

Scientists study fossils to learn about life long ago. They learn how different kinds of plants and animals lived millions of years ago.

When Animals Lived

By studying fossils, scientists have been able to learn when different animals lived on Earth.

4.6 billion to 600 million years ago	600 million to 245 million years ago

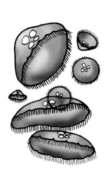 

Bacteria and simple animals

Fish and other sea animals

Scientists can tell how animals walked and if they lived alone or in groups by studying their footprints.

245 million to 66 million years ago	66 million years ago to present

Dinosaurs and the first birds and mammals

Mammals and humans

Scientists discover about seven new kinds of dinosaurs each year by studying fossils. With each new discovery, scientists learn more about past life on Earth.

While digging in El Salvador in South America, scientists found the fossils of 22 different animals.

The Fact Box

In 2001, the oldest known tick fossil was found. The tick was alive about 90 million years ago!

Scientists in California work to uncover the remains of a large mastodon (MAS-tuh-dahn). *It is believed that today's elephants come from mastodons.*

Glossary

bacteria (bak-**tihr**-ee-uh) very tiny living things that can usually be seen only through a microscope

buried (**behr**-eed) to have been covered, especially with earth

cast (**kast**) a fossil that has been formed in the shape of a plant or an animal by minerals from water

fossil (**fahs**-uhl) the mark or the remains of a plant or an animal that lived long ago

layers (**lay**-uhrz) thicknesses or levels of something that are on top of one another

minerals (**mihn**-uhr-uhlz) solid matter that comes from the earth

mold (**mohld**) an empty space that is filled with something that hardens and takes the shape of the space

scientists (**sy**-uhn-tihsts) people who study the world by using tests and experiments

sedimentary rock (sehd-uh-**mehn**-tuhr-ee **rahk**) rock that is formed by layers of sediment, which are pressed together over thousands of years

woolly mammoths (**wul**-ee **mam**-uhths) large, hairy elephants that lived about five million years ago

Resources

Books

Eyewitness: Fossil
by Paul D. Taylor
DK Publishing (2000)

Rocks, Fossils and Arrowheads
by Laura Evert
Creative Publishing International (2002)

Web Sites

Due to the changing nature of Internet links, PowerKids Press has developed an online list of Web sites related to the subjects of this book. This site is updated regularly. Please use this link to access the list:

http://www.powerkidslinks.com/ear/fos/

Index

Word Count: 424

Note to Librarians, Teachers, and Parents

If reading is a challenge, Reading Power is a solution! Reading Power is perfect for readers who want high-interest subject matter at an accessible reading level. These fact-filled, photo-illustrated books are designed for readers who want straightforward vocabulary, engaging topics, and a manageable reading experience. With clear picture/text correspondence, leveled Reading Power books put the reader in charge. Now readers have the power to get the information they want and the skills they need in a user-friendly format.